The Little Pumpkin Book

By Katharine Ross · Illustrated by Katy Bratun

Random House · New York

Text copyright © 1992 by Random House, Inc. Illustrations copyright © 1992 by Katy Bratun.
All rights reserved. Originally published in slightly different form in 1992 as
A CHUNKY SHAPE BOOK™. First Random House Junior Jellybean Books edition, 1999.
Library of Congress Catalog Card Number: 98-67347 ISBN 0-375-80106-5
www.randomhouse.com/kids

Printed in the United States of America 10 9 8 7 6 5 4 3 2 1

JUNIOR JELLYBEAN BOOKS and colophon are trademarks of Random House, Inc.

In spring, the children planted some seeds.

They watered…and weeded…

until the seeds sprouted...
one leaf...two...

and grew into a vine.
The vine bloomed.

Each blossom grew into a tiny pumpkin.

As summer wore on, the pumpkins

grew…

and grew…

and grew…

until one autumn day, they
were big enough to pick…

and carve!

What splendid jack-o'-lanterns!

Later, the children picked
more pumpkins...

to make pumpkin pie...

and pumpkin cookies.

But they saved just enough seeds to plant in the springtime.

The End

The End